Forbidden (L.O.V.E.) Attraction

by

Jakwontez Glover

The contents of this work, including, but not limited to, the accuracy of events, people, and places depicted; opinions expressed; permission to use previously published materials included; and any advice given or actions advocated are solely the responsibility of the author, who assumes all liability for said work and indemnifies the publisher against any claims stemming from publication of the work.

Dorrance Publishing Co
585 Alpha Drive
Pittsburgh, PA 15238
Visit our website at www.dorrancebookstore.com

ISBN: 979-8-88925-186-6
eISBN: 979-8-88925-686-1

Forbidden (L.O.V.E.) Attraction

"Adam was human just like the rest of us. He didn't want to have the apple just because it was there. He wanted it because he wasn't supposed to have it."

As I lay down in the bed next to him, wondering if he still loved me if I had bruises, all yellow and blue. Like the berries he had for breakfast in his belly that he chewed. Wondering if he would love the baby he put in me, against my own comfort. Like the zone he wouldn't leave for me. Would he like me more if I had a feverish attitude? Like the girls who made his eyes wander. Would his eyes composed of green and brownish gold turn me to stone? Like what would get thrown at me for speaking against him. Would he be more satisfied if I made a compromise? Like the sunrise we share. Would my meds work, and all this discontentment would fade? Like him touching me without overwhelming resentment wading within me. Would he find me hurting myself, would he stop me? Like when he found me in my head stabbing myself or will he let it be? Would you save me my love? Like how you saved those girls and got off to their sabotaging bodies of true yellow and blue bruises to my body. I wonder closing my eyes. As the morning approached my love greeted me with a kiss and breakfast in bed. I miss you this morning, I missed you yesterday, watching the sun shine. Here is what I have to say. For you I wish you an awesome day. Keep smiling and have an excellent day.

Good morning! I love you, my love. I love you too as tears raced down my face.

They say:

Love is like the wild rose-briar,

Friendship is like the holly-tree —

The holly is dark when the rose-briar blooms

But which will bloom more constantly?

Oh, how I love that man. I could remember the first time I met him I was sitting there, at my favorite secret spot, overlooking Lake Quinault. It's a hidden gem in Washington state owned by the Quinault Indian Nation and before that day, if I had my way, no one would ever sit and admire its handsomeness other than me. The lake, a destination point for fishermen, swimmers, and sightseers, is nature at its most spectacular. It is located deep in the Olympic National Forest. It isn't easy to find, even if you're looking for it. Once discovered, even the most magnanimous outdoorsmen will keep the secret to themselves. In an era where, too often, free time is wasted in front of a flat screen TV, Lake Quinault is a reminder of the reasons for taking vacations and the sunrise over the lake is God's definition of must-see. That particular trip occurred in early summer. I remember it vividly because I had to be in place just after 5:00 a.m. to catch the sun as it appeared over the mountain. Summer is the best time to watch the sunrise because no one in their right mind would be up early enough, nor would they be hardy enough to make the journey to my secret spot. No one except me.

"Is this seat taken?"

Not many people can remember the first words spoken by or to the love of their life, but I absolutely can. That morning, as I turned to see from where the unexpected voice was coming, the first light of dawn revealed the most handsome gentleman I had ever seen. Not all women might have thought so. That day I wore no makeup, a pair of ripped jeans, and a faded brown hoodie. Hair, perfectly auburn, looked as if it hadn't been touched since I rolled out of bed that morning. It was obvious I had made no effort to look beautiful and yet I had an inner spark that couldn't be hidden. Not by tattered jeans or a faded hoodie.

Something changed that first moment he saw me. I changed. I had spent years guarding my secret spot, and now, surprisingly, unexpectedly, delightfully, I wanted nothing more than to share my sunrise with him.

I, unfortunately, was not born a poet and as such the most romantic thing I could think of in response to his inquiry was, "It's a free country."

With that, he invaded my secret spot, both next to the lake and in my heart. The silence that followed was both loud and revealing. He wasn't there for small talk; he was there to admire the beauty of the sunrise. We sat in silence and watched as the sun peeked over the horizon, covering the two of us in its warming light. He and I carried on a conversation without words. He told me, silently, that he understood the importance of the moment, and I responded in kind that this moment was made all the more special because he was there to share it.

Perfection is a goal impossible to realize in this mortal realm, but that morning came as close as is humanly possible. So many thoughts ran through my mind as the sun revealed itself completely. Then just as quickly and quietly as he had come, I rose to my feet, wiped some residual dirt from the seat of my ripped jeans, and headed down the trail and out of his sight. Eight words verbalized; an infinite number of potential events contemplated. Thirty minutes had passed, a lifetime had been imagined. I was sure I would never see him again, and the thought made me overwhelmingly sad.

The next five years came and went, five long years since that day at the lake. There were first dates, first kisses, and the words "I love you" exchanged. Yet every time fate or intention would reach down and sabotage a promise. I became determined to find peace in my solitude. There was always a reason or an excuse for my ending every potential relationship, but at its core was a shared sunrise and a conversation that didn't happen. I went to our spot from time to time, to see the sunrise, not for him. At least, that's what I told myself. I had given up without realizing I was hoping. Hoping to see him again. Hoping to feel what I felt that day. Hoping he would be there.

And then it happened. It was once again summer, it was sunrise, but this time he was there.

"Is this seat taken?"

"It's a free country."

The same eight words.

At the time, I didn't know that he, too, had often made the trip back to our secret spot. Seeing him again, I knew I wouldn't let the opportunity slip from my grasp, not a second time. When the sun had completed its part in our play, I rose to my feet and wiped the dirt from my jeans exactly as I had done five years earlier. This time, however, he stood up as well.

"My name is Joshua, Joshua MaCoy. I don't like coffee, but I'd really like to have a cup with you."

"My name is Angela, Angela McClain," I responded, matter-of-factly, "and I would be glad to share a cup of Joe."

I called it Joe? It's funny the things that confirm that love is real. I couldn't tell him that day, for fear of losing him, but at that moment, I was sure. I had said "I love you" to others before, but it was obvious to me that I had lied. For in that moment, I was finally sure what love felt like. Lifetimes are only lifetimes when viewed in reverse. A cup of coffee became a dinner date. A dinner date became a commitment. A commitment became a proposal, and a proposal became forever. There were kids and dogs and vacations, but more than anything, there were trips to Lake Quinault. Always at sunrise. Always just the two of us. Never any words spoken. You never know the last time is the last time until it's too late.

The final trip we took to Lake Quinault was like all the rest. It took a little longer for tired, old bones to make the trek, but we found our spot, sat together, and conversed in silence. The sun, unaffected by time, rose as perfectly as always, but he rose only with my help.

"Would you like to share a cup of Joe?"

He knew I did. He knew sitting next to me pretending to like coffee was my greatest pleasure. He also knew he would never come back to see another sunrise even though I was too stubborn to admit it to myself. That day in the café, we told stories of family and friends, living and lost, as we sipped on what had eventually become my favorite beverage. We made a mental scorecard of our life and realized we had won.

Two days later, I lost him. Just like that first day at the lake, I watched him as he left me alone, this time without even the hope of returning. The sadness I felt from years back flooded over me like a tidal wave. *I'll save a seat for you.* Those were his last words to me.

True to myself, I replied, "It's a free country."

Then, he was gone.

One day, hopefully soon, I will watch the sunrise with him again only from a far better secret place. Until then, I only go to our special spot at night. I'm never alone when I go there. I make my way to our clearing and sit down just as I did all those years ago. As the moon reflects off the lake, I feel his comforting hand. Those were the good ole days.

"Well, I'm off to work. I hope you have a wonderful day," as we exchanged hugs and kisses.

"Don't wait up, I have a big project that my secretary and I are working on," disappearing out the door.

"Wait. What? Nevermind. I love you hunny," holding him close.

"I love you too, baby, but I have to go," rushing out the door.

Before I could say another word, he vanished.

As I began my wifely duties, an empty condom fell onto the floor as I was making the bed. I picked it up and stared at it for a moment. *Sigh.* I don't know what to feel anymore. I feel like something isn't right. *Angela, get it together you're overreacting he loves you he wouldn't do anything to hurt you. Relax. I don't know, I can't shake that feeling. I must go confront him at work.*

As I made my way to his job looking in the window, I saw something that made my heart shatter to pieces. My husband was making love to another woman. I fell on the floor clutching my heart, crying, and beating my head with my hands. *That son-of-a-bitch, how could he do this to me? That's ok, karma's a bitch,* as I gathered myself.

I sat in the living room, taking a pull of my cigarette, waiting for him. Before I could take another pull of the cigarette, he entered as if everything was okay.

"Oh hunny, you scared me. What are you doing up?"

I just stared at him as if I didn't have a soul. My mind wouldn't allow me to sleep.

"How was your day at work?"

"It was okay. I got a lot of work done."

"Oh okay," I said with a grin on my face, pulling on my cigarette.

"Working on that project really put a lot of stress on me. I think I need to relieve some stress," as he tried to approach me.

"I think you had enough stress-relieving," I mumbled under my breath.

"What's that hunny?"

"Nothing. Anything for my king as I strolled to the bedroom."

As we made love, all I could think of was how could I get back at this son of a bitch. Two minutes in and he was done.

"That's it?" I said rolling over, rolling my eyes.

No response. I looked over and he was sound asleep sucking on his thumb. The look on his face makes me disgusted. At that moment your girl put her plan in motion... Karma is a bitch!

Forbidden (L.O.V.E.) Attractions

"The worst pain is getting hurt by a person you explained your pain to"

Three years earlier.

"God, I hope I get this job. This can be life changing," he said as I adjusted his necktie.

"Baby I'm sure you're going to be great."

"I hope so, we can't afford to miss another rent payment," as a tear fell from his eyes.

I did what a queen would do… uplift her king. "Let's pray about this."

We did so.

Lord, thank you that you have entrusted me to manage and steward my finances with wisdom and diligence. Help me to grow in wisdom as I seek to honor you through my finances. Help me to budget my money well, work hard, and save the resources you have given to me. I'm asking in your name father. Amen.

"Thank you, baby, I needed that," as he got up, walking out the door.

I waited until he left to dial my mother for help. She answered the phone after the third ring.

"Hey baby, how's the married life?"

"Not good, Mother. Maxwell got laid off and with him having a criminal record, it is kinda hard to find something."

"I feel your pain. I had to go through the same thing with your father. Angela, you can do better."

I sat silent on the phone as my mother preached to me. "But Mom, Maxwell is my husband and I love him. I'm going to stay by his side. Why do you hate him so much? You could at least give him credit for trying to get a job… you know what, don't worry about it."

I figured it out before she could get another word in. I hung the phone up.

Three seconds later there was a knock on the door. As I raced to the door, there was an eviction letter waving in the wind. As I opened it, my eyes began to flood.

YOU HAVE THIRTY DAYS TO COME WITH THE MONEY OR WE ARE THROWING YOU OUT.

I fell on my knees, screaming out to God. I screamed so loud that my neighbor rushed out of his house wondering if everything was ok.

"Are you ok?" he said, running toward me.

I got up and said, "Yes, I'm ok thanks."

"Is there anything I could do?"

I wanted to say yes, but I didn't want anyone in my business. "No thank you," as I made it in the house.

At this point, my life was over. Maybe my mother was right. I deserve much better. *Agggh*. I had to shake that negativity off. He didn't give up on me when I was going through a lot. I'm going to be there for him. That's what a wife is supposed to do. As I gathered myself, I began to feel weak. I made my way to the couch. Instantly, I was dead to the world. As I slept, God came to me in a twilight dream. God took a loved one once. She was amazing and beyond anyone earthly. Our first born that we lost in 2009. She had eyes that sparkled with universes, but she needed something else. She needed to leave. Now God is left to his own devices, making failure after failure, creature after creature, person after person. Children that grow to be adults reflecting not God's unending power and omnipotence, but his sorrow and imperfections and his heart. God doesn't have a plan... he has an idea and a vague one at that as it is. We are god. We are all little pieces of our creator and his punctured heart.

It got so deep that I began to cry. "Lord, help," as I cried out.

It felt as if I was in a coma. A dream I will never wake up from. I sometimes catch myself separating myself from the world, but I have to remind myself I am part of the universe! For I am part of the universe, and the universe is part of me. For whatever my body does, my spirit will be forever free! As I woke up, I tried to clear my head and thoughts started racing in. I started to question everything and regret every sin. I think of all my failures, every detail of what I did wrong. After hours of relieving pain, I convince myself I don't belong.

Suddenly feeling isolated, I balled up in a nearby corner. The silence never ended. I felt like I would never escape. There's too much I just can't mend. I felt overpowered and worthless, like I'll never do anything right. I just hide till the world fades away.

As I made my way to bed, I realized a new day had come. It's time to put on a brave face. I put those negative thoughts away until I return to this place. My eyes begin to connect. I was awakened by keys jiggling. My husband entered with a grin on his face.

"What's wrong?" as I sat on the edge of the bed.

"I didn't get the job."

"Why?"

"Because of my background. Everybody makes mistakes. I paid for mine a long time ago. I'm sorry, baby."

"God is going to bless us," rubbing his shoulder. "When one door closes, another one opens. We just gotta have faith."

"I know. This could have been a breath of fresh air," burying his face in his hands.

"It's alright. Maybe this wasn't the job for you. I mean, you are an intelligent guy with a good head on your shoulders."

"Anyways, enough about me. How was your day?"

"Terrible."

"Terrible?"

"Yes."

"Why? What happened?"

"Even though you told me not to worry my mother about our problems..."

"Okay, go on."

"Well, I waited until you left then I called her."

"Why would you call h..."

"Baby, we needed her help," as tears rolled down my face. "Plus, we got an eviction letter stating we have thirty days to come up with the money or else."

"Or else what? What do you mean or else?"

I handed him the letter. "Baby they are throwing our stuff out," bursting into tears.

"Fuck," he yelled as he slammed his phone on the table. "Something's got to give," balling his hand up.

I began to soak his shirt due to crying.

"I have to make a phone call," as he grabbed my chin, aiming for a closer kiss.

"No, you are a changed man. Things will get better," as I pulled back.

"But as a man, I have to provide."

"But..."

"But nothing. I'm sorry," looking into my flooded eyes as he walked out the door.

"No," I screamed as I fell onto the floor crying.

It was too late. He was gone. I felt my life come crashing down. That part of my life begins to restart. I instantly fell into depression mode.

"Mother, I need you," as she answered my call.

"Wha... wha... what's wrong?"

"Everything is wrong. Maxwell is up to no good."

"I told you you deserve better," she said after explaining what happened.

"I know but you have to let me learn."

"Okay," as she sighs. "Let's pray," as she calms my depression.

Lord, Help me Lord to not give in to a mindset of my own making but arrest my thoughts as they venture there. I need Your undertaking for I am weak at times, my God. And my burdens I try to bear when You have told me take each burden to the Lord and leave them there. Help me seek Thy face each day. In the early morning hour and when I do I know You are pleased, I want to know Your power/ Praise God for Thy Holy Spirit, a Comforter indeed. For when I am at my darkest moment, Your grace supplies my need. Take an x-ray of my heart. Show me where I falter. Then bring me to that quiet place before Thee at Thy altar. And in praising recognition for what You've done for me, here I am again, O Lord. Thank God for Calvary! Amen.

"Thank you, Mother. I needed that."

"Anytime, I'm always here for you. I love you."

"I love you too, baby. Now get some sleep."

Three hours later, I was awoken to police banging on my door and SWAT teams aiming at me with heavy weapons through the window.

"Oh my God, Maxwell. What have you done?"

"Ma'am, get your hands up," as they rushed in, pushing me onto the floor. "Where is he?"

"I... I don't know what you are talking about," as I panicked.

"Don't play games with me. Angela, you know I can make your life a living hell," pointing the gun at my temple. "I'm going to ask you again, where is Maxwell?"

"I told you I don't know. Fuck." Angela paced back and forth.

"You are going to give me information on him. NOW."

I just sat there, silently staring at him as if he didn't have a soul.

"Fine. Since you don't want to cooperate, take her ass down to the station. Maybe you would change your mind when we charge you with harboring a fugitive," spitting out his cigarette, laughing.

"Go to hell," I said as they locked my hands together rushing me out the door.

Life is hell. Give it back, and then some. There is far too much light in that soul, sass in that step, and determination in that heart to ever let a horned devil win. Why do you think you've been given hell? Even he knows a queen when he sees one. Make him bow. As we made our way to the station, I was greeted by two fat detectives.

"Hello Angela, how's life treating you?"

"Fine," I said with a smirk on my face.

"It seems like you have some important information that you want to share with us."

"What are you talking about?" in confusion.

"Come on, Angela. You know what we're talking about."

Confused. We spent hours arguing. After two hours they gave up and charged me with "harboring a fugitive".

Three hours later. I made bail. I made it home. I instantly called him.

"Maxwell, Maxwell pick-up the damn phone."

My call was unsuccessful after trying five times.

"Dammit," I said, slamming the phone down.

I sat, wondering how I got myself into this situation. Then it hit me. I remembered hearing him on the phone talking about a plan that he had in motion and when I walked in, he instantly hung up and tried to comfort me as if he was covering something.

Damn I feel stupid. I thought he had changed. I don't know why I took him back.

Memories started to play in my head. I remembered you left me for someone that didn't want you. I had no choice but to let you go. But you released me, and I healed, and I feel stupid for regretting letting you go. I knew they wouldn't love you like I do and didn't think about you like I did. You tore me up and used me like I was nothing and you forgot me to go to those who don't know you. You completed me, but I'm still here even though you're gone, and I feel stupid for thinking you were the one. Fuck. They won't love you like I did. How can I be so stupid? Momma was right, as I turnt up a shot of vodka. Then passed out on the couch.

I suddenly awoke to the doorknob turning. Instantly I jumped up. grabbing the pistol that was hiding underneath the couch cushion. Pointing it at the door, ready for whatever. The door opened, revealing my husband as he rushed in.

"What the..."

Before I could finish, he interrupted me. "Woah.. Baby, where did you get that gun from?"

I stared at him as if he didn't have a soul, pointing the gun at him. "Do you care to tell me what's going on? You got the police kicking down my door questioning me about the whereabouts of you. Then they charged me with harboring a fugitive."

"Wait... what?" he said, looking confused. "Baby, I went out for a couple of drinks to clear my head."

"Maxwell, tell me the truth."

"Baby..."

I knew he was lying so I made a single shot.

At that moment he became nervous. "Bbbbaby, I'm telling you the truth. I love you. I wouldn't dare lie to you."

"But why did the police..."

Before I finished, his phone started to ring. Both looking at the phone, I noticed it was a number I had never seen before.

"Who's calling you?"

"Oh baby, that's nobody but Jason. He didn't want anything," he said, laughing.

"Well, aren't you going to answer it?"

He looked at me, panicking. "Baby, I told you it's nobody important. You are important right now."

I became frustrated. "Maxwell, pick up the phone," holding the gun steady.

"Baby please," he tried to plea.

"Maxwell, don't play with me and answer the damn phone. Don't you love me?"

"Yes, I love you."

"Okay. answer your phone."

Nervous, he picked it up. "Hello."

I could hear the other person. "Baby, why did it take you long to answer the phone? I thought you were going to Mcdonald's so I could feed our unborn child."

That moment, he knew he fucked up. I aimed the gun at him, shooting him in the leg.

"What the fuck?" he said as he fell on the floor, dropping the phone near the couch.

"Get the hell out of my house you dirty dog," as he cowered to the couch.

"Oh, don't think you're getting away with this."

Before I could finish, the police busted through the door. *Another Black Woman Gone Crazy.*

"Freeze. Don't move. Drop your weapon," the policeman screamed, pointing his gun at me.

"Well, well, well Mr. McClain, we've been looking for you."

"For what?" he said.

"You know, the murder of the elderly woman at the grocery store."

"I don't know what you are talking about."

"Stop playing damn games with me."

"Do I look stupid to you? Does it look like I was born yesterday?"

"I've had enough of his nonsense. Get them out of here," the detective snapped.

"Fuck," Maxwell said out loud.

As we got transported down to the jail my husband started to cry. I kinda felt bad for the bastard.

"Baby, I'm sorry.

"What?"

"Sorry for what I said. I'm sorry that I got you in this mess. I shot and killed that elderly woman."

My mouth dropped. "What the fuck?" I said in shock.

"Yes, I'm sorry baby. I'm sorry for all the drama I put you through. I'm sorry I got another woman pregnant too. I'm sorry for everything. Can you forgive me?"

"Maxwell... I don't know what to think. I had your back throughout the years. I even stuck up for you when my mother said you were no good. And for you to go behind my back and destroy me... Maxwell, I don't know," as a tear fell down my face.

"Baby, I'm sorry."

"It's too late Maxwell. I don't love you anymore."

It's such a hurtful feeling when your spouse tells you they don't love you anymore.

"Damn. I've messed up," as we made our way into the jail.

They separated us.

"Well, well, Mrs. Angela McClain, we meet again," Detective Richardson said with a smile on his face. "So, Mrs. McClain, I see that you just got out of jail on bond due to harboring a fugitive."

"Yes, that's bullshit and you know that. I had no knowledge my husband was a fugitive," I snapped.

"Come on now Angela, do you expect me to believe you that you had no knowledge that Mr. McClain was a fugitive?"

"Yeah. Why would I have a fugitive stay with me?"

"Good question," Detective Richardson said as he slammed his folder on the table. "You know I can revoke your bond and send your ass to jail. It's in your best interest to tell me what I need to hear."

I got nervous and started to think about my life, biting my nails. "Okay. What do you want to know?"

"Everything, starting with the night Mr. McClain committed murder at the grocery store."

"Mr. Maxwell McClain, glad to see you again."

"What do you want from me?"

The detective started to laugh. "We got your wife in the other room. I know you don't want her to throw her life away over your nonsense."

"No."

"Good. Now tell me what I need to hear."

"What do you want to know?"

"The murder of that elderly lady at the grocery store."

"I don't know what you're talking about," Maxwell snapped.

"Come on Maxwell, what kind of fool do you take me for?"

"A dumb one."

Both the detective and Maxwell laugh.

"I see you have a sense of humor."

They both argued for nearly four hours. The detective gave in due to not getting Maxwell to confess.

"We are going to see those going to get the last laugh when you are doing life behind bars," as he slammed the door walking.

After two hours. the detective came back and played the video the night of the robbery. After seeing himself shooting that elderly woman, Maxwell hung his head with his face in his hands.

"Fuck you." Maxwell screamed.

The detective sat down next to him, saying "Are you ready to talk?"

"Yes." I started to break down and cry. "Look. All I know is that my husband had a plan in motion. What was the plan? I don't know. When I caught him, he instantly hung up the phone and started to kiss me. Then we made love. After waking up, he was gone. I tried calling to see where he went but I got no answer."

"I think she's lying," the other detective said.

"Mrs. McClain. that's bullshit and you know that stop playing games and tell me the truth."

"What the fuck? I'm telling you the truth. Why would I lie?"

"That's your husband, the only man that cares about you. Angela, why would you cover for someone that doesn't give a damn about you? You know I can send you back to jail on new charges. You don't want that now, do you?"

"I am telling you the truth," I said as my eyes begin to fill with tears. "You know what, I'm tired of trying to explain myself. I'm done. I want my lawyer."

"You know what... fine. Fuck," as he slammed his hand on the table. "I'm tired of playing games with you," as the detective stormed out the door.

Throughout the troubles we faced, they charged me with aggravated assault with a deadly weapon and harboring a fugitive, receiving a five-year prison sentence while my husband got life in prison for the murder of that elderly woman. Fuck, I got a record.

After serving two and a half years, I was free. All I could think of was my mother's conversation she had with me before everything took place. I hate to admit she was right all along. I should have listened to her. All this would have been avoided. But no, I was in love with a dirty dog… Maxwell McClain. The man who destroyed my life. I hated him so much that I wished he would die in prison, but I had to learn to forgive him.

Matthew 6:14-15, "For if you forgive other people when they sin against you, your heavenly Father will also forgive you. But if you do not forgive others their sins, your Father will not forgive your sins.

At least that is what Pastor John once said. Once in a blue moon I receive letters from him. On how he was sorry for all the trials and tribulations he put me through asking for forgiveness.

Dear Angela McClain,

I'm sorry for all the pain I've caused you. I never meant for that to happen. You were just the only one I trust. I know sorry can't take away all the pain and harm I've caused you. I have no excuses because it is just cowardly to give you an excuse that will never help. I love you and I'm sorry. These tears that run down my cheek are filled with sadness and hurt because I loved you so much and now, I know that it will never work. I messed up and now I see that you mean the absolute world to me. I know sorry's not enough because I'm such a screw up. But for whatever it's worth, I wanted to say that you cross my mind every single day...

The thought of you makes me smile, and I know our love was real, so I'm writing you this letter so that you know how I truly feel. What I really want to say is that I'm sorry. I know that you didn't deserve to be hurt like that, and I know that you will find someone who will love you and treat you right. They will make you happy and that person won't hurt you like I did.

So I'm so sorry for everything I've done. All I have to say is that I love you and I'm so so sorry. I hope you can find it in your heart to forgive me. I hope to get a chance to see you.

Sincerely,

Maxwell McClain

After reading his letter, my eyes instantly fill with tears.

"I've forgiven you," folding the letter. "Even though you put me through a lot, I will always love you. You are my king and I'm your queen. I'm forever the MRS. MCCLAIN!"

"Wait... what am I saying?" pausing for a minute.

Memories of him cheating on me started to replay back into my mind.

"Baby I cheated and I'm sorry. I cheated on you."

Now I don't know what to do. I want to come clean to you but instead I keep lying to you. I really didn't mean for it to happen. I should've said no but I got caught up in the moment. I acted like nothing happened because I love him. But how could I love him, considering he cheated on me? If only you knew what I was going through, then I wouldn't have to lie to you. I wouldn't even cheated onyou. I've been keeping it from you and that is going good but it's only making it worse because when you find out or when I can finally tell you, it will only make things worse and really hard to deal with.

Baby, I'm so sorry that I lied to you. I'm so sorry that I cheated. You found out because I said the wrong thing. I tried to lie my way out, but you knew exactly what had happened. I lied, you cried. I felt so bad and depressed you were all torn up inside wondering why I'd do such a thing. I had no answer or excuse because there wasn't one. I got caught up in something I couldn't get out of but now that is all in the past. I am now proud of the fact that you found out, even though it was the worst way and that I had done it anyway. But we worked it all out we got past it. For some odd reason, it made our relationship stronger. Don't ask me why, don't ask me how. But there is one thing I will tell you. That is, don't cheat on the one you love because I almost lost mine and trust me that sucks. I would have died if we would have been over.

Baby, I learned my lesson. I'm sorry. I love you, Angela McClain.

I instantly snapped back to reality. Fuck him. As I made my way out the door, my phone started to ring. I glanced at it for a moment. Fuck. "California Department of Corrections". Maxwell.

"Hello."

"Hello, this is a prepaid call from Maxwell McClain, an inmate at California Department of Corrections. To accept charges, press 1."

Instantly, we got connected. Hastily, I said hello. Before I could get another word in, he took over.

"Hello baby, how are you doing? I hope life treats you well."

"Yeah, it is," I said.

"That's good. I miss you. Do you miss me?"

There was a long pause.

"Yeah."

"I haven't heard from you in a while. Have you been receiving my letters?"

Yeah Maxwell, I have."

"So why haven't you been writing me back?"

"I've been busy."

"With life, right?" he said, laughing.

Silence.

"Angela, look, sorry for making you mad. Sorry for everything. I said sorry for lying to you sorry, I'm so sorry. Sorry if I disappointed you, sorry if I hurt you, sorry for everything."

Before he could say another word, I interpreted him. "Maxwell, you said enough, and you did enough. Yeah, I forgive you for the things that you did to me. When I was in prison, I once hated you, but I learned to forgive and forget. I also learned that you can't make it to the kingdom of heaven with hatred in your heart."

"That's right, thank you," he said as he began to cry.

"Maxwell, it's okay. Let me say a prayer for you. **Father, I want to live in the shadow of Your wing. When life is hard, and I don't know what to do, help me remember that You are with me and that I am never alone. I cannot live without You. I cannot face tomorrow without the promise of Your presence. Today I choose to walk and live under the protection of You, the Most High. In Jesus' Name, Amen."**

"Thank you, baby."

Before we could finish our conversation, the phone call ended. I sat down on the couch and started to cry. My mother saw me sitting on the couch crying.

Sitting next to me, she proceeded to hug me. "Baby, what's wrong? Are you ok?"

"No, I'm not.

" Tell me what's wrong."

"It's Maxwell."

"What about him?"

"I'm still in love with him. Even though he destroyed me he will forever be my king."

"Wait… what that I'm hearing?" as she pushed me away. "Angela, are you serious? All the things this man put you through, you still love him?"

"Momma, you don't understand."

"I understand, Angela, well. You are free. He is in prison. He's not getting out. You need to get a divorce and find someone else."

"But Mom..."

"'But Mom' nothing. Angela, you got a second chance to correct your life. You have your whole life ahead of you," wiping the tears from my eyes.

"Mom, you're right."

"Angela, I just don't want you to throw your life away again. All I want is what's best for you."

"Thanks, Mom, for understanding."

As my life is finally coming together, I found the man of my dreams. Joshua. Joshua MaCoy. Joshua was a big-time lawyer at Johnson & Johnson Law Firm. He knew about my situation with me and Maxwell. He put his action in motion where I granted a favorable final divorce. I was happy at that moment, even though I still was receiving letters from Maxwell.

On July 23, we got married and God blessed us on May 5 with a beautiful angel by the name of Aniyah Ava MaCoy.

I was living life until I got a phone call from prison stating that my ex-husband was murdered.

"Oh my God what happened?"

"Mr. McClain was found dead. Dead and alone."

"MURDERED."

There was nobody near when the outcast died on his pillow of stone. Not a friendly voice to soothe or cheer, not a watching eye or a pitying tear, —Oh, the city slept when he died alone in his cell on a pillow of stone.

"I'm sorry Mrs. McClain."

"It's okay, I said as I started to cry."

"If you need anything. feel free to contact the warden at (310)555-0000."

"Thanks."

As my husband entered returning home from work, he sensed his queen weakening. He dropped his briefcase and started to nourish his queen.

"What's wrong with my love?" lifting my chin.

"Nothing," I said in despair.

"My love, I know your heart. I feel its weakness. What's wrong?" kissing my lips.

"It's my ex-husband."

"Maxwell?"

"Yeah."

"What happened?

"He was found dead this morning."

"Oh wow. I'm sorry to hear that. How did he die?"

"Someone murdered him."

"Damn. Prison can be a world inside itself. Did they contact his family?"

"Yeah."

"I'm sorry baby," comforting me.

"It's okay."

Tired of life and longing to lie peacefully down with the silent dead, hunger and cold and scorn and pain. The life of Mr. Maxwell McClain! After I found out about his death, I made plans to go to New York to comfort his family. As I laid down in bed, reading the last letter he wrote me filled my eyes with tears.

Dear Angela McClain,

My heart desires, the one I love. I love you so much, and I just can't believe we are still together after the turbulent and trying times. You are my hope and you will be in all my dreams and aspirations. You are my yesterday, today, and tomorrow. I fall in love with you when we are together, and I fall further in love whenever you are far away from me. You are my perfect love, the reason why I love LOVE. You are good luck for me in everything I do. Whenever you are here, I feel love; whenever we are apart, I feel love. You made me see that love is not just about loving, it is all about showing love. I truly appreciate how far we have come, and I promise to love you forever.

Today, you need to realize that you are the best thing that ever happened to me. You are a blessing and your worth is greater than all the gold in this world. I can not compare how wonderful you are to my life and everyday I see reasons why we are just meant for each other. Darling, I am stuck on you like a leech, not in a bad way but in the best way possible. You made me see that life is worth living when there is love in it and I see life in your love. I am still battling with words to show how much you mean to me right now, but could only come up with this. All I know is that our love story is going to be the most exciting and passionate ever. I promise to love you forever.

I know I am going to spend the rest of my life worshiping you for all the goodness and sweetness you have brought into my life. You have given me every reason to want to continue to appreciate your love and this I promise to do forever. Listen, I promise to give you all of me, because all of me wants all of you. I know that you are not perfect and I promise to love you forever, my perfect imperfection.

I remember the last time I had a dream with you in it. You took me to the heights of perfect loving, heights that I never wanted to come down from. We have had our fair share of misunderstandings, but this has made us more perfect for each other. I have grown so used to you that you seem like the faraway sister that I grew up with. I love you more every day, because you are everything to me, and after all these years of being together, I promise to love you forever.

Sincerely,

Maxwell McClain

My daughter was awoken from hearing my cries.

"Momma, what's wrong?"

"Nothing baby." I hate lying to my daughter.

"Momma, something is bothering you. I know it, I can feel it. I'm your twin," hugging me.

"It's my ex-husband, Maxwell. He died in prison. Murdered."

"Oh my God. I'm sorry, Mom. I hope everything will be ok."

"It will."

"Well, try to get some sleep," as she kissed my forehead.

"Ok baby."

"I love you, Mom."

"I love you too baby," I said as she walked back to her room.

I folded his letter, placing it back into the envelope as I rolled over and went to sleep.

His funeral was very different from any funeral I'd ever been to. After they lowered his casket, each one of them put a shovelful of dirt over him. I remember crying so hard I felt weak. My husband saw my weakness. He held me so tight that you thought a snake had grabbed me. My cheeks burned from the tears.

"It's okay, baby," as he wiped the tears from my eyes.

My whole body was shaking as I picked up the shovel, but I'm glad I didn't do it. When Maxwell and I first started calling one another, I thought it would be more than a burden on me, but I was completely wrong. I learned so much from him. He gave me more than I could ever give him. I will never forget him or the talks we had. I know that I must never take anything for granted, especially my health and the gift of life!

From ashes to ashes, from dust to dust. You'll rise again, in this I'll trust. You're in our hearts, 'till the end. We will meet again, depart my friend. You may be gone, but I know you're near. In my heart, I hold you dear. My only hope, in peace you'll rest. I still miss you, I bet you guessed. I'll see you soon, it's a must. Ashes to ashes, dust to dust.

Rest In Peace: **Mr. Maxwell Jadyn McClain**.

That night I was comforted by my husband and daughter.

In my dream, he came to me.

"You think I've gone, that I am dead, and life has lost its will. But look around, I am right there, living with you still. I watch your tears, I feel your pain – I see the things you do. I weep as well, each time you cry. My soul, it lives with you. It gives such joy to hear you laugh and do the things you do. And when you smile o'er bygone days, I smile right with you too. For we're still one, just you and me, one mind, one soul, one being. Walking forward into life, though only you are seen. And in the stillness of the night, when the pain really starts. Stretch out a little with your mind and draw me to your heart. For I am always right in there, always by your side. For you have been, all my life's days, my joy, my love, my pride."

My husband heard my cry. He rolled over and cuddled with me, whispering sweet tunes in my ear and kissing me at the same time. Then we made love.

The next day, I woke up to breakfast in bed. My husband did his thing. Gosh, I will forever love this man. He knows what to do to make my day better. On the side of my pillow was a love letter from my king along with a picture of him. It reads:

Dear My Beloved Queen,

If I were to tell you how much I am in love with you, days and nights would pass by. You are the reason I believe in the power of love. I never thought that I could love anyone this much until I met you. Now that you are with me by my side, I have become a better person. Thank you for being with me and loving me with all your heart. I promise to take all your woes away and be with you now and forever.

Your darling hubby,

Joshua MaCoy

Oh my God, I swear I love this man as tears raced down my face. I was so much in love that I forgot I didn't have panties on but a see-through shirt. Dancing throughout the house listening to some Marvin Gaye, "Sexual Healing".

"Oh my word, Momma," Aniyah said, bursting into the kitchen.

I couldn't do anything but accept the fact that my own daughter caught me off guard. I tried to cover up but it was no use. She saw everything with her grown ass.

"What? Don't act like you've never been in love before," I said, taking a sip of orange juice.

"I have, but not that much."

"Well, when you get a little older you will understand."

"Whatever you say mother. I'm not trying to be late for school. Are you going to take me to school?"

"Yeah, I take you."

"Well, hurry up, Mom," Aniyah said, walking out the kitchen laughing.

Later that night, I was ready for my man to come home. Aniyah was over at her friend's house for the night. I had everything in order. Candle light dinner and a soothing bubble bath with the TheHE Temptations playing in the background. Waiting for him with his favorite see-through gown on, laying on the couch. Ten minutes later, my king came home. I greeted him at the door with a kiss on the lips then proceeded with the candle lit dinner, standing behind my king as he ate, rubbing on his chest and then little kisses on his neck. Not giving him a chance to change out. Fuck. I was horny at that point.

We made love in the shower. Cool water streams down upon our hot, sweaty bodies. Leaning my head back, the water falls upon my face. His hands caress the roundness of my full breasts. With his thumb and forefinger he squeezes my nipples. A moan escapes from my sensual lips. Slowly, his hands move down to caress my stomach. A surge of electricity runs through my body. Though we are in cool water, our bodies are on fire. I close my eyes and my mind wanders. thinking of him as my lover's hands move to my inner thighs. Slowly, I move it up to my womanhood. His breathing becomes more rapid, my body tense. As his fingers begin to lightly rub me, dreaming that he is kneeling between my legs. His strong fingertips are touching me, my body is enraptured by the dream. He finally stands and begins kissing me. His hands rub all over my dripping wet breasts. His hands encompass my silky butt cheeks. I surrendered to the thought of excitement. Driving my fingers deeply between my soft lips. The memory of our lovemaking drives me to heights. His fingers rub and caress quicker as he gasps hard. The electricity fills my loins and in flames my senses. I scream as the orgasm overwhelms. Fuck. That was some good sex.

As we laid in bed, I caught him texting another female. At that moment, I felt betrayed, but I didn't want to start an argument. He was my king, and I was his queen.

"Baby," I said, leaning on his side.

"Yeah?"

"You love me?"

"Of course I do. Why do you ask?"

"Nothing, just curious."

"What's the matter, baby? Talk to me."

"It's nothing, baby. Don't worry about it."

"Baby, please tell me what's wrong."

"Fine. I just saw that you weren't paying me any attention, but more to the text you received."

"Oh baby, it's just my new secretary. We were talking about this new upcoming project."

I kinda don't believe him. Memories of my late husband cheating on me.

I paused for a minute. "Fine, I believe you."

He felt like he had to plead his case.

"Baby, stop. I trust you. Now let's go to bed."

"Okay," as he kissed me on the lips.

Two hours later, I woke to him texting on the phone. When he heard me move, he instantly put his phone down.

"Baby, what are you doing?" I questioned.

He hesitated, "Ummm, my mother."

"Really?"

"Yes, you know how my mother is."

"Whatever Josh, go back to sleep."

I waited for him to be in a deep sleep. Finally, he was out. I reached over, got his phone, and went through it. I found stuff in it that would make a bitch go crazy. That son of a bitch. *How could he?* I thought, putting his phone back. I got something for his ass.

As the morning approached, he greeted me with a kiss and breakfast in bed.

"I miss you this morning, I missed you yesterday watching the sun shine. Here is what I have to say. For you I wish you an awesome day. Keep smiling and have an excellent day. Good morning!"

I wasn't in the mood for his nonsense. I just laid there.

"What's wrong, baby?" he said, trying to be all romantic.

In my mind, I said: "You know what you did, stop playing games."

"Oh, nothing babe, just not feeling good today."

"I hope you feel better," he said as he laid next to me.

As we lay next to each other, I wondered if he'd still loved me if I had bruises all yellow and blue. Like the berries he had for breakfast in his belly that he chewed. Wondering if he would love the baby he put in me against my own comfort. Like the zone he wouldn't leave for me. Would he like me more if I had a feverish attitude. Like the girls who made his eyes wander. Would his eyes composed of green and brownish gold turn me to stone? Like what would get thrown at me for speaking against him. Would he be more satisfied if I made a compromise? Like the sunrise we share. Would my meds work, and all this discontentment would fade? Like him touching me without overwhelming resentment wading within me. Would he find me hurting myself? Would he stop me? Like when he found me in my head stabbing myself or will he let it be? Would you save me, my love? Like how you saved those girls and got off to their sabotaging bodies of true yellow and blue bruises to my body.

I wonder, closing my eyes. *Whatever.*

11:30 rolled around. He jumped up rushing, trying not to be late for work.

"Well, I'm off to work."

"I hope you have a wonderful day," as we exchanged hugs and kisses.

"Don't wait up I have a big project that my secretary and I are working on," disappearing out the door.

"Wait. What?"

"Nevermind."

"Ok, I love you hunny," holding him close.

"I love you too, baby, but I have to go," rushing out the door.

Before I could say another word, he vanished. As I began my wifely duties, an empty condom fell onto the floor as I was making up the bed. I picked it up and stared at it for a moment. *Sigh*. I don't know what to feel anymore. I feel like something isn't right. *Angela, get it together you're overreacting he loves you he wouldn't do anything to hurt you. Relax.* I don't know, I can't shake that feeling. I must go confront him at work.

As I made my way to his job looking in the window, I saw something that made my heart shatter to pieces. My husband was making love to another woman. I fell on the floor clutching my heart, crying, beating my head with my hands. *That son of a bitch, how could he do this to me? That's ok, karma's a bitch,* as I gathered myself.

I sat in the living –room, taking a pull of my cigarette, waiting for him. Before I could take another pull of the cigarette, he entered as if everything was okay.

"Oh, hunny, you scared me. What are you doing up?"

I just stared at him as if I didn't have a soul. "My mind wouldn't allow me to sleep. How was your day at work?"

"It was okay. I got a lot of work done."

"Oh, okay," I said with a grin on my face, pulling on my cigarette.

"Working on that project really put a lot of stress on me. I think I need to relieve some stress," as he tried to approach me.

"I think you had enough stress –relieving," I mumbled under my breath.

"What's that, hunny?"

"Nothing, anything for my king," as I strolled to the bedroom.

As we made love, all I could think of was how could I get back at this son of a bitch. Two minutes in and he was done.

"That's it?" I said rolling over and rolling my eyes.

No response.

I looked over and he was sound asleep, sucking on his thumb. The look on his face makes me disgusted.

At that moment, your girl put her plan in motion. Karma is a bitch.

As I made my way to the bathroom, I stopped and grabbed the pistol that was hiding under the bathroom sink. Cocking it and hiding behind my back, I made my way back to the bedroom where he was sound fast asleep. I pointed it at his temple.

"Baby, baby," I said, kicking him.

He woke up in surprise, a gun pointing at him. "What the hell is going on?"

"You know what is going on."

"Baby, I don't know what you are talking about."

"So, what happened at work today?"

"Nothing happened but me and my secretary were…"

"You mean your (secret)ary."

"Wait. What?"

"Yeah. you heard me. That bitch is more than your secretary."

"What are you talking about Angela?"

"Come on man, you know what I'm talking about. You're fucking her."

"Wait..."

Before he could finish, I interrupted him. "I found a condom in our bed and to top it off, I went by your job and saw you and her fucking."

He couldn't say anything but hang his head. "Baby, I'm sorry. I didn't mean to hurt you."

All of a sudden, his phone started ringing.

"I wonder who that can be?" I said dramatically, Both of us looking at his phone. "Well, are you going to answer it?"

"No."

"Answer the damn phone," as I became more furious.

"Baby, it's nothing."

I instantly shot one round in the ceiling. "I'm not playing with you Josh. Answer the damn phone."

"Okay, okay," he said in fear, picking up the phone.

"Put it on speakerphone."

"Baby no, please don't."

"Shut up, you don't make the rules, I do. Now put it on speakerphone," as I punched him in the face.

"Hhh... Hello…"

"Hey baby, why do you sound like that?"

"No reason, just a little busy at work."

"Oh ok, whenever you get done, are you still going to come over?"

"I.. I.. I don't know what you are talking about."

"What do you mean Josh?"

Before he could say another word, I jumped in on the conversation. "Wooooow, Josh so is this what you are doing?"

"Josh, who is that?"

"I'm his wife."

"What?"

"Yeah, his wife."

"Oh my God. Josh, you told me you were single."

"He lied to you."

The poor girl was so hurt that she didn't want anything to do with them anymore.

"You know what Josh? I quit and I'm reporting you."

"Please don't destroy my career."

"You ruined it yourself. Fuck you, Josh," as she hung up the phone.

"Wow Josh, you are in a bad situation. I can't believe you lied to her. What makes it worse is that you betrayed me, and I told you from the beginning, don't play with my heart."

"Baby, I'm sorry."

"Shut up Josh, I don't want to hear it. Stand up."

"What?"

"You heard me. Stand up."

"Why?"

"Just stand up."

"Ok," as he got up.

"Now strip."

"What?"

"Do as I said," pointing the gun at his dick.

"Okay, okay."

"I want you to eat my pussy."

As he began to eat out my pussy spreading my legs wide open. Diving, flicking, searching amongst my pussy's flaps, It's the nectar of the goddess it wants. I want to lap. Tip of your tongue on my clitorus, probe around my hood. Waves of sex run over you. It makes me feel real good. My juices run in your mouth, as you suck in every precious drop, then your fingers get inside, begging you not to stop. Like a bear grabbing honey, scooping juice right out my minge, whilst your tongue danced up and down, my pretty flowers fringe. Gliding on the edge of my lips, waiting to raise my hips, allowing your tongue deeper, so I get longer sips. Tongue deep inside my hole, fingers beating on my clit, tongue dance to fingers beat, played upon my slit. My body arching up and down, as I begin to cum, I hands pushing your head on deeper, whilst I hold you by the bum. Grinding myself faster, your tongue keeps my pace, juice running everywhere, I soaked your mouth and face. Then with a gasp and scream, orgasm rips right through my soul, a shuddering climax I have cum, and I've achieved my goal.

Laying on my back, motionless on the bed, I slide myself beside you, I gently stroke your head. You turn around to face me, you have that "just cum" grin. You stroke my face so tenderly, wiping juice right off your chin. Pulling you close, I kiss you. We lay in love's embrace, I can't help to grab a glance at you and see your face.

"I love to taste your pussy. I just love to eat you out, making you so satisfied is what love is all about," he said.

"Oh, do you?"

"Yeah, you have the best pussy. I can eat you all night."

"Hmmm," I said, pulling up my clothes.

Before he could say another word, I shot and killed him close range. Blood spattered everywhere. Even on my face. I got nervous. I never killed someone before. I panicked. I ran in the bathroom, scrubbing my face as if I was trying to change my skin color. Racing back to the bedroom where his body was resting on the floor. Instantly. I dragged him by his legs, placing him in the shower, and rinsing away the blood. Changing my clothes, I called my mother, the only person I could trust at this moment.

Ring... Ring... Ring...

"Hello."

"Mama, I killed someone."

"What?"

"I murdered my husband."

"Oh my God, Angela, why?"

"Momma, he played with my heart. He cheated."

"Oh my God. Angela, what are you going to do?"

"I don't know. Mama, I'm afraid."

"Go to the police."

"No, will they know I am the murderer? I'm burying his body somewhere not far. Now dead men tell no tales. Mama, I killed someone..." I began to panic.

Dropping the phone, I fell on my knees and started to talk to God, crying. Crying, "Lord, please forgive me. I need your grace to make it through. All I have is you, I'm at your mercy. Please forgive me, I am so sorry Lord. I would love to turn back time to change my mistakes. Please help me to be forgiving of myself, and to move on from this place. I feel overwhelmed by regret. Please wash away this emotion with your grace. I know you love me, and understand my heart. Please fill me with your strength and courage as I resolve to live for You."

Before I could finish my conversation with God there was a knock on the door. I slowly got up walking toward the door with the gun tucked in my back pocket. Loaded.

"Hello," I said, peeking through the peephole.

"Hey, this Tom, your next-door neighbor."

"What the fuck do you want?"

"I heard some gunshots. I thought I came over to see if everything was okay."

"Yeah, everything was fine. It was just my television."

"Oh okay, sorry to disturb you."

"You're fine. Have a good day," as he walked off my door.

"Fuck. That was close," as I took out a cigarette.

I began to question myself. "What the fuck am I going to do with his body?" I asked myself. I just get some trash bags and put his body in it. As I proceeded to hide his body, my daughter walked in on me.

"Oh my God, Mother, what the hell are you doing?"

She startled me. Turning around, I could see the disappointment in her eyes.

"Baby, it's not what you think."

"Then tell me what that is."

Before I could explain, she interpreted me. "You know what? I'm calling the police."

"9-1-1, what's your emergency?"

Before she could say more, I shot her. My eyes begin to fill. Falling on my knees next to her as her blood cried out for help. What the fuck had I done? My only daughter. Dead.

The neighbor heard the gunshots. Instantly, they called the police. Ten minutes later, the house was surrounded by police. Talking on their megaphone, trying to get me to surrender as I sat on the living room floor, rocking my daughter's dead body, crying, asking God for forgiveness. I began to pray.

"I am sorry my Lord, forgive me for my sins. I did not come to you as early as I thought. My love of the material world kept me away from you. But now I realized the value of your goodness. Please bless and accept me in your shelter. I am sorry my Lord, forgive me for my sins. I did not listen to your precepts that were presented to me. My evil soul kept me away from you. But now I realized the power of your words. Please bless and accept me in your shelter. I am sorry, my Lord. Forgive me for my sins. I did not visit your church or worship places. My depraved mind kept me away from you. But now I realized the worthiness of your love. Please bless and accept me in your shelter."

As I finished my final thought. I took the gun from my back, placed it to my temple, and pulled the trigger. I'm gone. Dead.

The police heard the shots and they rushed in the door. All were surprised. It was too late. I was already gone.

"Fuck," they said as they placed their hands on their head.

I'm free. In heaven with my daughter.

Channel 2 covered the story.

"Breaking news from Channel 2. Authorities rushed into the home of Mr. and Mrs. McCoy late Thursday after gunshots in the home and having a standoff with Mrs. McCoy for nearly the hours. Upon entering, they found both Angela Charlotte McCoy

(50) and daughter Aniyah Ava McCoy (17) lying on the couch, both pronounced dead. Well as Mr. Joshua Amadeus McCoy (52) dead in the shower. According to the neighbors, The McCoys were good people. Very friendly and hardworking people. The only time you see them is when they go to work. And their daughter, Aniyah Ava MaCoy, was a very loving person. Straight A student and captain of the cheerleader team. As you can say, "beauty with brains" This is Jessica Gomez, news reporter, signing off."

As you could say: "ANOTHER BLACK WOMAN GONE CRAZY". The death of me and my family was so devastating that it spread like a wide fire throughout the community. Even my mother was devastated. People would walk up to her asking questions and taking pictures as if she was some celebrity. I kinda feel bad that I left her in this situation. The day of my death, I didn't tell her how much I love her. But, Mom, I killed someone.

If I could relive my life over again, my child would be the most important thing to me. I'd make up for the times when promises were broken. And tell her all the things that went unspoken. I'd always be there, as a good mother ought to be. I give my daughter the best. God's love in me. As I watch over my mother, protect her and be a true guide. And ask for my forgiveness for all the times I lied. I tell her I am sorry for the pain I caused her in the past. And when I say I am sorry, ask for my forgiveness. I'll ask if I need no excuses to justify my mistakes. I would admit my wrongs, that caused their hearts to break. I'd shower upon them my devotion and love and gently woo their attention. Upon the Father above I do the things mothers and daughters do. And tell them of a wondrous God who makes their dreams come true. I tell those things I had hidden in my heart from the past, plant godly wisdom. A precious seed sown at last. And when I say I am sorry, it means, I'm sorry, I'll never hurt them again. For they'll know what it means to be born again, reborn.

It's too late to turn back. For those who are still breathing, thank God that you are still alive. You get a second chance in life. Repeat after me.

Lord, I thank You God for most this amazing day for the leaping greenly spirits of trees and a blue true dream of sky; and for everything which is natural which is infinite. I who have died am alive again today, and this is the sun's birthday. This is the birthday of life and of love and wings and of the gay great happening illimitably earth. How should tasting touching hearing seeing breathing any—lifted from the no of all nothing—human merely being doubt unimaginable. I had that chance. I blew it. I allowed Satan to take control of my life. Life can be hard sometimes, but it's going to be okay. Sometimes we see things that aren't meant to be seen. Sometimes things aren't always as they seem. Sometimes we need someone to call our own, especially when we're alone. Sometimes people just can't understand why things get out of hand. Sometimes life just isn't fair, especially when people just don't care. And sometimes it's hard to say, why things have to be this way. Sometimes it's all you can do to get by, especially when dreams continue to die. Sometimes it's nice to sit in the rain. Even to just relieve the pain. And when we've had a really bad day, sometimes we just need to get away. We never know what's wrong without pain. Sometimes the hardest thing and the right thing are the same. And sometimes when people get hurt, even the strongest ones may need comfort.

My mother once told me growing up to learn while still a child what this life is meant to be. To know it goes beyond myself, it's so much more than me. To overcome the tragedies, to survive the hardest times. To face those moments filled with pain and still, manage to be kind. To fight for those who can't themselves, to always share my light. With those who wander in the dark to love with all my might. To still stand up with courage though standing on my own. To still get up and face each day even when I feel alone. To try to understand the ones that no one cares to know. And make them feel some value when the world has let them go. To be an anchor, strong and true, that person is loyal to the end. To be a constant source of hope to my family and my friends. To live a life of decency to share my heart and soul. To always say I'm sorry when I've harmed both friend and foe. To be proud of who I've tried to be and this life I chose to live. To make the most of every day by giving all I have to give. To me, that's what this life should be to me, that's what it's for. To take what God has given me and make it so much more to live a life that matters to be someone of great worth. To love and be loved in return and make my mark on Earth. Until this day that left a mark on my life.

Six years after my death, there was a book and movie made based on my life. It was called *Forbidden (L.O.V.E.) Attractions*. When my mother found out, she was surprised and at the same time happy. I guess she wanted to spread awareness on marriages. Later. she was elected leader for the community. I must say that I'm proud of her finishing her master's degree in Family and Marriage Counseling. She even got married. She often comes by and visits me at my graveside, telling me all the things that she had accomplished in life. I wish I was there to celebrate with her. She even wrote me a sweet poem.

Dear my sweet precious daughter,

How are you? I am always thinking of you and praying that wherever you were in this world you would just be happy. For all these years I have asked for your pardon. I asked God to punish me for my sinful act. But it seems that my voice is unheard. My plea is unnoticed. Today the bridge of my patience and pain has collapsed and so I have decided to reach you. I need to talk to you, my baby. You remember the very first day of your arrival? When I told your father that we are expecting you. We were so happy. I was brimming with emotions of happiness. I felt at the top of this world, the same way I felt when your father came into my life. But this was more than that. A perfect joyous moment. We had already decided your name. If you would have been a baby boy, then we would have named you Arun and if you would have been a baby girl, we would have named you Angela Avant McCoy which means 'from the land of God'. I have a confession to make. Before you were born your father got me pregnant at the age of fifteen. You had an older sister, but we agreed to get an abortion. You don't know all this? But then that catastrophe. Your grandparents took you to the hospital. Your father was crying and pleading with me not to do this. At that moment, I didn't have a choice. I was a baby myself. Plus, I was in pain. They all were praying that we don't want you in our life. That devil examined you. There was a biological sort of picture of yours on his screen. Somewhere in the depths of my heart I felt happy for you. I felt happy that you'll be my princess. My beti! I knew that you were a girl before that criminal doctor told me. It was as if you were speaking to me in your innocent and angelic voice, telling me that, "Momma, I am coming into this world, your baby. But Momma, I don't feel safe here. Please take me home.'

"She is a girl. What do you want to do with her? Do you want to abort her? Extra charges are applied if you want us to bury her."

Oh God! Those dreadful words. I was shocked to hear them. My body was paralyzed. He as telling me to kill my daughter. I was very angry, but it was your father's mistake too that he and my parents agreed to take me there. I am sorry, beti. I decided to take your sister away, to take her home. But my parents stopped me. They had already decided your sister's fate. They tried to kill her. Take her from this world. But they already decided before her entry into this world. I could not think anymore. It was as if someone stole my soul from my body. She wouldn't be able to see this world, to play with those toys that I brought for her, to eat those candies, to make friends, to fall in love, to marry. Everything and every single dream of mine which I had dreamed for her was shattering. And then she was gone from my life, from our life. I never forgave your father, and he also went with her. I am sure you both are in heaven and your grandparents and you are taking good care of your sister. I am happy that I got a chance to be your mother.

Beti, after all these years I still miss you. I'm glad you came into this world. But my weakness for that moment made me a killer. I am your sister's killer, beti. I killed her and I'm sorry for what I have done. I am very sorry, beti. I will not die, beti. I won't kill myself because that would be an easy death and not a punishment. I will suffer through all this.

I am sorry Angela. Please forgive me, your mother!

Love your mother,

Mrs. Evelyn Jaylani Smith

She started crying. She placed the letter on my headstone along with a dozen roses. All these years, how could she lie to me? Having a sister? Wow. I was in shock. But hey, this world is a cruel place. The story of my life.

The moral of this story is: Failing to make certain sacrifices and adjustments are some of the common reasons why marriages don't work. One of the greatest marriage lessons from most failed marriages is that relationships require work from both partners. Nonetheless, they shouldn't be hard all the time. Relationships are indeed complicated and are not always rainbows and butterflies. There are bumps in the road that will test your commitment and love. Successful marriages are made when couples are willing to sort things out, compromise, and go the extra mile to resolve marital issues. Even if you are already married, you and your spouse must continue to do something extra to keep the spark and chemistry alive. A little room for patience, understanding, and compromise can benefit your marriage. Learn to make personal sacrifices and make your spouse feel appreciated and valued. Nevertheless, trying to make your relationship work should not be hard all the time since marriages are meant to be enjoyed.

Forbidden *(L.O.V.E.)* Attractions